It's Thanksgiving,

Jane Smith

Albert Whitman & Company
Chicago, Illinois

OAK

It's Thanksgiving!

Thanksgiving is a day to give thanks for all the good in the world.

Every year, my family picks apples for my mommy's special stuffing.

My daddy, little sister, and I play football in the backyard. We make autumn wreaths with colorful leaves to decorate the front door.

Today is the big Thanksgiving celebration! We'll have a feast with all the trimmings: turkey, green beans, sweet potatoes, apple stuffing, corn bread, and everyone's favorite—Grammy Ella's famous pumpkin pie.

All our family and friends will come over to celebrate together: Grandpa Joe, Grammy Ella, and my best friends, George and Mary Margaret, and their families!

"This year Chloe Zoe is my official pumpkin pie helper!" announces Grammy Ella.

"Really?" I ask her. The pumpkin pie is the most important part of the feast.

"Yep!" She winks. "It's going to be the best pie ever!"

Grammy Ella and I gather the ingredients: pumpkin, cream, sugar, eggs, and spices.

"Look for *a* for allspice, *b* for black walnut extract, and *c* for cinnamon," says Grammy Ella.

POPPY SEEDS

Cayenne

Vanil

Cinnamon

BLA
pepp

I find the first two spices easily, but there are two jars with
the letter *c*. *Which one could it be?* I make my best guess.

Grammy Ella carefully measures the pumpkin, cream, and sugar into the mixing bowl. I crack the eggs—1, 2, 3. Then we add the spices.

"Hmm…this cinnamon smells funny," says Grammy Ella.
"But look—*c* for cinnamon," I say, pointing to the label.
Grammy Ella leans closer, squinting. "OK!" she says. "Let's get
this pie in the oven."

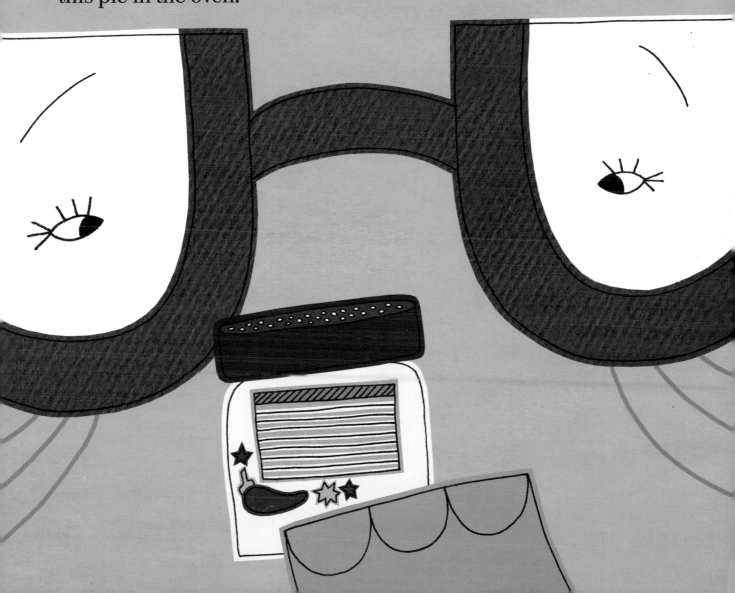

Grammy Ella and I clean up while the pie is baking. The oven beeps just as the doorbell chimes. George and Mary Margaret are here!

"Happy Thanksgiving!" cheers Mary Margaret.

"Yum! What smells *so* good?"
asks George.
 I point to the pie, now cooling.
"The pumpkin pie!" I beam.
"I helped make it!"

It's time for the Thanksgiving feast to begin. Everyone gathers around the dining room table.

We all take turns saying what we are thankful for:
family, friends, peace, love, candy, and everything pink.

GEORGE

MOM

MARY MARGARET

CHLOE ZOE

GRAMMY ELLA

"Let's eat!" laughs my daddy. Everyone piles their plates high with delicious food.

"Save room for dessert!" Grammy Ella winks at me.

"Oooh! I can't wait to taste the pie Chloe Zoe made," says Mary Margaret.

"Me too!" call out George, Grammy Ella, and my whole family.

GRAMMY ELLA

CHLOE ZOE

MARY MARGARET

GEORGE

When everyone is finished, my mommy cuts
a slice of pie for everyone and tops each piece
with whipped cream.

I take a big bite and—BLAH! The pumpkin pie is spicy hot! Gross! I look around the table. Everyone is spitting out their pie into their napkins!

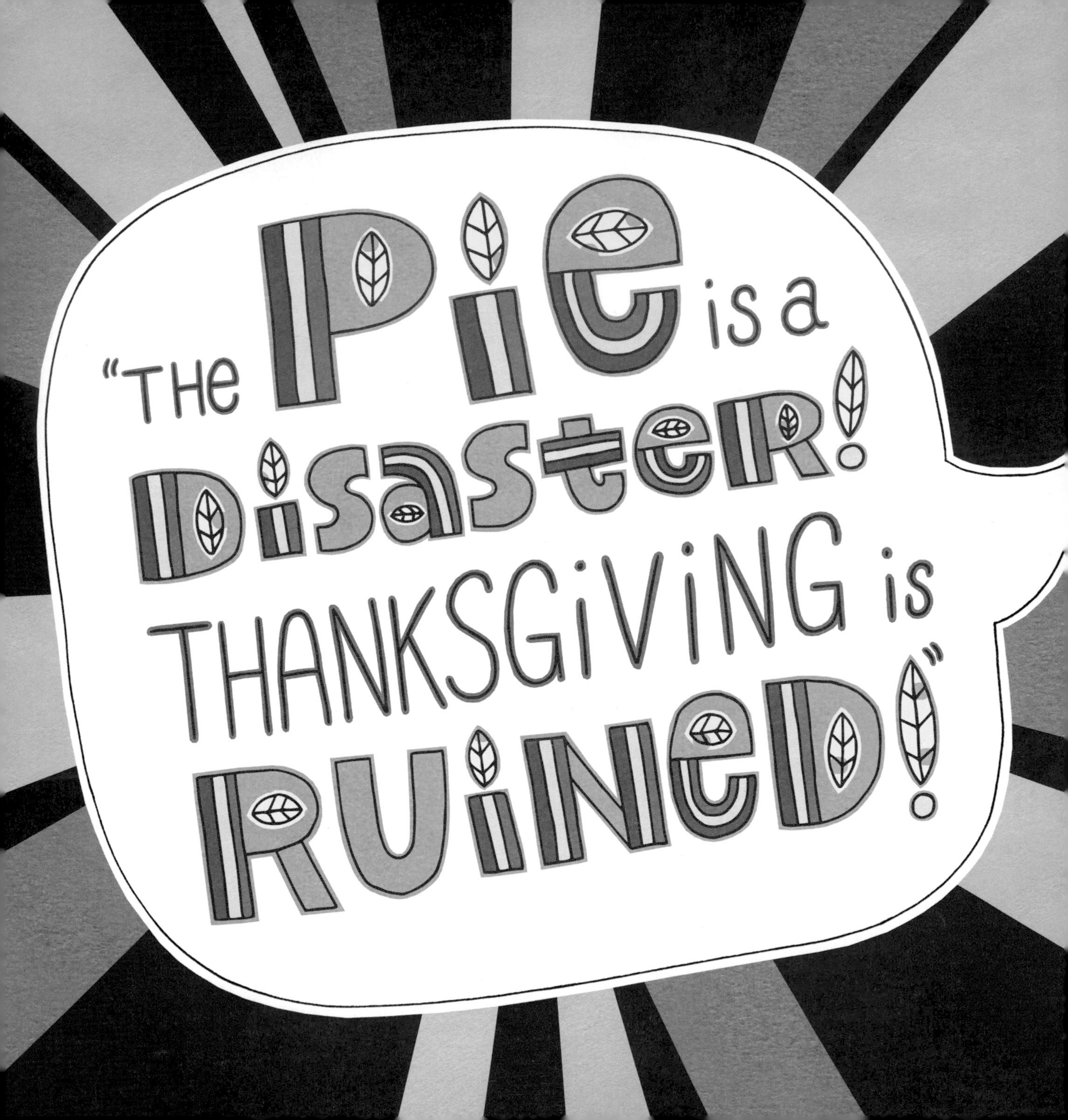
"THE PIE is a DISASTER! THANKSGIVING is RUINED!"

My whole body starts to shake. I burst into tears and run to my room.

There is a soft knock on my door and Grammy Ella comes in.
"I'm so sorry I let everyone down," I sniff.
"Oh, Chloe Zoe, you didn't let us down," says Grammy Ella.

She wraps me up in a big hug. Mary Margaret and George peek around the door and run over to hug me too.

"You know, Chloe Zoe," says Grammy Ella,
"The best part of Thanksgiving really isn't the pie."
I look up in surprise. "It isn't?" I ask.
"The best part is being together."

"We miss you," says Mary Margaret.
"Please come back."

"Your mom has vanilla ice cream!"
says George.

I smile at everyone and nod.
"OK, let's go!"

When we get back, my daddy is holding the *c* spice jar. "I think you two accidently put cayenne pepper in the pie." Grammy Ella and I look at each other in surprise.

"Well, I like the extra spice!" says Grandpa Joe.

Everyone laughs! "Happy Thanksgiving, Chloe Zoe," says Grammy Ella.

For more Chloe Zoe fun
—like crafts, coloring pages, games, and activities—
visit www.albertwhitman.com.

For Lisa—I am forever thankful for you.

Also available:
It's Valentine's Day, Chloe Zoe!
It's Easter, Chloe Zoe!
It's the First Day of Preschool, Chloe Zoe!
It's the First Day of Kindergarten, Chloe Zoe!
It's Halloween, Chloe Zoe!

Library of Congress Cataloging-in-Publication data is on file with the publisher.

Text and pictures copyright © 2017 by Jane Smith
Published in 2017 by Albert Whitman & Company
ISBN 978-0-8075-1212-8
Printed in China
10 9 8 7 6 5 4 3 2 1 LP 22 21 20 19 18 17

Design by Jordan Kost

For more information about Albert Whitman & Company,
visit our website at www.albertwhitman.com.